I0712755

ANITA'S UNDERWATER EXPLORATION

CARING FOR OUR OCEAN

By
Krystine Cabrera

Illustrated by
Guilherme Salomon

Published by Krystine Cabrera 2023

Anita's Underwater Exploration
Copyright © 2023 by Krystine Cabrera
Cover by Guilherme Salomon

Printed in the USA.
All rights reserved.
No part of this book may be reproduced,
transmitted, or stored by any means, electronic,
mechanical, photocopying, recording, or
otherwise, without written permission from the
author. For information regarding permission, all
inquiries should be directed to
www.storiesbykrystine.com

ISBN-13: 979-8-9875454-3-0 (Hardcover)
ISBN-13: 979-8-9875454-2-3 (Paperback)

I WOULD LIKE TO DEDICATE THIS BOOK TO THE VAST AND MAGNIFICENT OCEAN, AND TO ALL THE WONDERFUL CREATURES THAT CALL IT THEIR HOME.

THANK YOU TO ALL THE LITTLE ONES THAT ARE LOOKING TO PROTECT AND PRESERVE OUR OCEAN FOR YEARS TO COME.

- KRYSTINE

Hi there! This is Anita, a Junior Park Ranger. She wants to earn an Underwater Explorer badge with her friends.

"It's a beautiful day for some fun and adventure!" Anita said with excitement. "Today, we are going to dive underwater! Let's see what sea life we can find!"

"The ocean is filled with underwater resources like plants and sea critters. To earn our badge, we need to learn how to protect them because they keep our climate regulated, and provide us air to breathe and food to feed us," Anita stated.

"The next thing we have to do is make sure the environment is as clean from litter as possible," she continued, "Let's go take a look!"

Putting on their wetsuits to keep them warm, the friends slipped on their fins, masks, and air tanks that will allow them to breathe underwater.

"Down into the ocean, we go!" Manu exclaimed.

And together, the friends dove into the deep blue sea.

The kids found a colorful coral reef filled with all kinds of animals and sea plants.

"Oh! I see a seahorse!" Farah pointed out.

"Yes, so pretty," Anita agreed, "but be careful to not step on or touch the coral reef! This can hurt it and impact the sea critters because that is their home."

As the kids continued to dive even deeper, they noticed an old rusty tin can on the ocean floor.

"Look at this!" Manu pointed. The kids swam towards the tin can to pick it up.

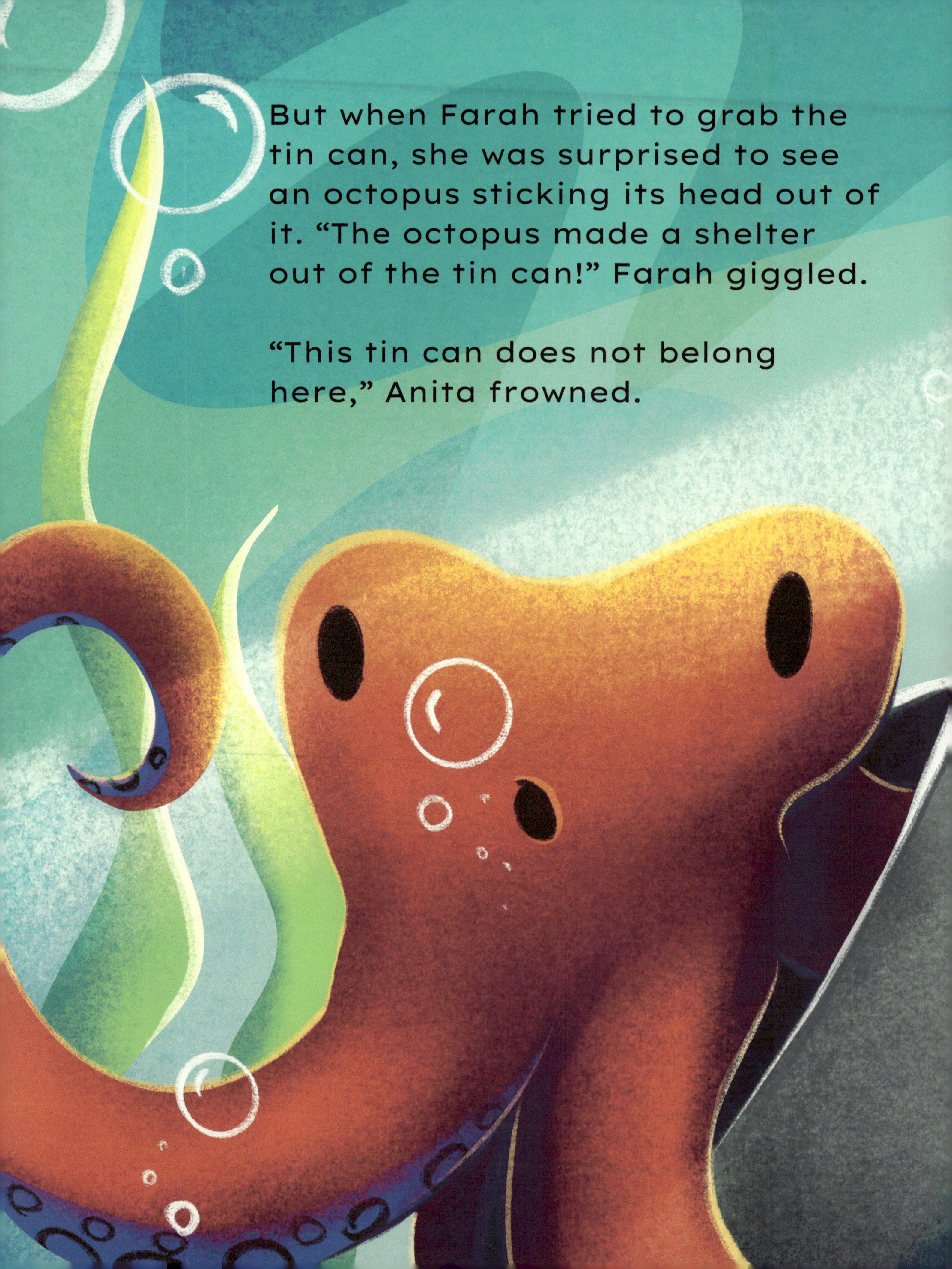

But when Farah tried to grab the tin can, she was surprised to see an octopus sticking its head out of it. "The octopus made a shelter out of the tin can!" Farah giggled.

"This tin can does not belong here," Anita frowned.

Manu agreed. "Octopuses use litter as shelter when their natural resources become scarce due to humans collecting them to sell."

Manu found a shell, picked it up, and placed it next to the octopus. "There you are, my friend!" he said joyfully. "That's much better now!"

The octopus swam out of the tin can and fitted itself into the shell as the kids cheered. Farah quickly grabbed the tin can and stuffed it into the net she brought along.

"Litter can expose these animals to toxins. We can't let this be used again as a shelter," Farah said.

"Oh look!" Manu said with excitement. "Jellyfish!"

In awe, the kids swam toward the jellyfish.

But as they swam closer, the kids discovered that they weren't seeing jellyfish. They were seeing plastic bags. Even a dolphin had one stuck to its fin as it swam.

"Poor dolphin!" Anita cried out. "Why do we have so much trash in our oceans?"

The children swam to the plastic bags and stuffed them into their nets.

"Animals that eat jellyfish mistake this plastic for food," Farah worried.

"Well, let's keep on the lookout for litter!" Manu said, looking at the ocean floor.

Swimming with excitement, the
kids couldn't wait to see what else
awaited them underwater.

They were amazed at the different colored fish, crabs, shells, starfish, and dolphins swimming around them.

Manu pointed towards rocks that were lying on the ocean floor. "Look! I think I see a sea turtle!" he beamed while grabbing Anita's arm.

As they swam closer, they were saddened to find the turtle stuck to a fish line that was being held down under the rocks.

Acting quickly, Manu untangled the
fishing line as Farah pulled it out from
under the rock.

Now freed, the turtle happily swam away.

"We did it!" Farah cheered.
"Look at her swim!" Manu smiled, relieved.
"Such a beauty," Anita said in amazement.

At the end of the day, the kids were back on the boat.

"We are a step closer to getting our badge!" Anita exclaimed.

"To earn your Underwater Explorer badge, the last step is to share what you have learned," Richard announced. "Can you tell us what you all have learned?"

"I learned that the coral reef houses so many different species of animals and plants! It must be protected!" Anita answered.

"We need to use less plastic. Even when we throw it away, it can still end up in the ocean and harm animals," Farah replied.

"What else?" Richard asked.

"Plastic is tough and is used for short-term things but stays in the environment for a long time. It hurts our sea life," Manu explained. "Instead of using plastic bottles, we can use bottles made out of glass or steel instead."

"Yes! And instead of plastic bags, we can use reusable ones," Anita added.

"Congratulations!" Richard
announced. "You all have learned
so much about how every one of us
can help save our oceans and our
sea life."

Richard continued, "Anita, Manu, and Farah, you are our new Underwater Explorers!"

Everyone applauded as Richard gave them their new badges.

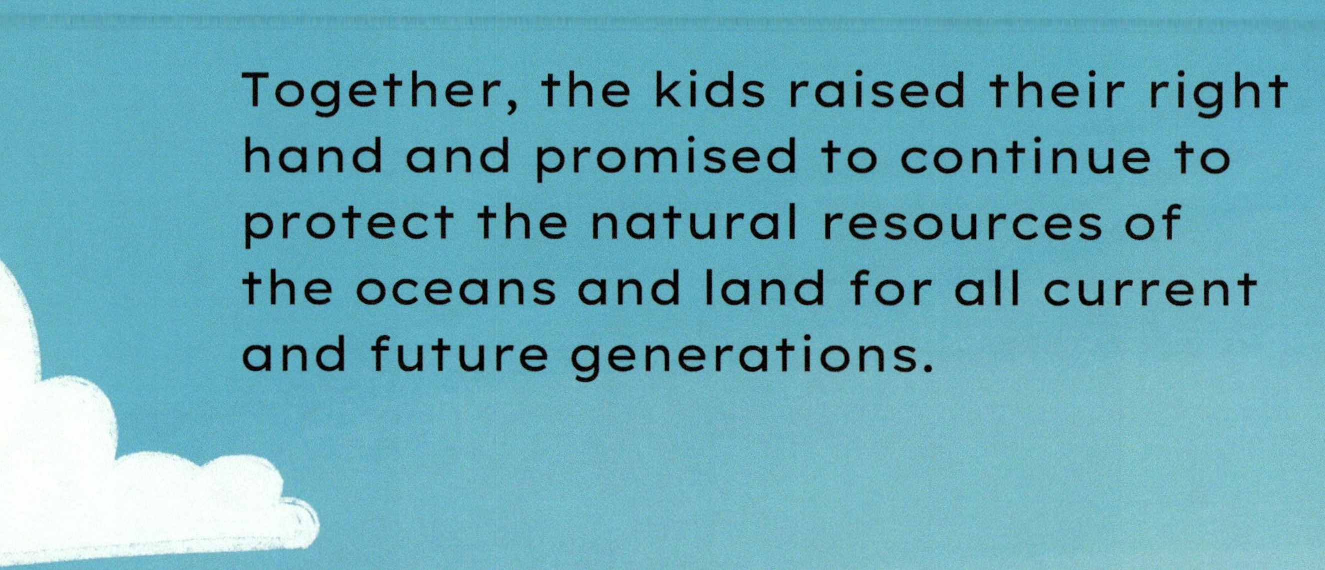

Together, the kids raised their right hand and promised to continue to protect the natural resources of the oceans and land for all current and future generations.

They promised to do their best to
keep the environment free from
litter and to continue to teach
others about the sea.

"This isn't the end!" Anita grinned. "If we work together, we can keep the ocean a beautiful place."

GLOSSARY

<u>Climate</u>: the weather pattern of an area over time or years.

<u>Coral Reef</u>: an underwater colorful and bright environment that shelters many sea animals and is made up of tiny creatures.

<u>Environment</u>: a surrounding area of a living person, animal, or plant.

<u>Litter</u>: things that end up in the environment that do not belong there which may injure animals and people.

<u>Toxin</u>: a poisonous substance that can harm humans, animals, or plants.

<u>Regulated</u>: to control or manage according to a rule.

<u>Resources</u>: a tool or material that is utilized to meet a need.

<u>Scarce</u>: when there is a lack of needed resources.

<u>Short-term</u>: an event that happened in a short period of time.

IF YOU LIKED THIS BOOK, READ THIS!

ABOUT THE AUTHOR

Krystine Cabrera was born in Seattle and raised by her Filipino father and half-Filipino, half-Caucasian mother, who instilled in her a passion for education. As a child, Krystine was an avid reader and enjoyed crafting stories of her own.

Drawing on her personal experiences, Krystine now writes to motivate and empower young readers to positively impact their lives and the world. Her latest work aims to inspire parents to involve their children in litter cleanup efforts, hoping to create a cleaner and healthier planet.

WANT TO GET INVOLVED?

Are you looking for ways to make a positive impact in your community? Anita and her team of Junior Park Rangers have created engaging activity sheets that you can use when you're on your cleanup adventures. These resources are available for free at www.storiesbykrystine.com, and they are filled with fun and engaging activities!

In addition, Anita offers an exciting opportunity for showcasing your commitment to the environment. By sending a picture of yourself practicing eco-friendly habits, it will be featured in the Junior Park Rangers' exclusive HALL OF FAME. This feature is a great way to motivate others and display your efforts. The process is simple; send the picture via email to:

hello@storiesbykrystine.com

Taking care of our environment is important, and we're so glad you're part of it!

ACKNOWLEDGEMENTS

I would like to take this opportunity to express my heartfelt appreciation to Eevi Jones for her invaluable guidance and mentorship over the past year. Without Eevi, this book would not be possible because her feedback improved the language and imagery I desired for this book. I am also deeply grateful to my long-time friends Terra Hoy, Bryton Martin, Jay Swartz, and Jasmin Williams for their continued support over so many years. Additionally, I would like to extend my sincere thanks to my co-workers Dennis Williams, Katherine Nahoi, Catherina Munoz, Sasha Myers, Ike Garcia, Tyere Garcia, Debrapang Garcia, and many more for their love and encouragement as I pursue my passion for writing. I feel incredibly blessed to have Sara Belarmino, Mariah Massengill, Brentley Sandlin, and Armando Molina Gómez be my pillars of support and for teaching me so much. To Mr. Bodach for teaching me the importance of picking up litter when I was in high school. And last but not least, I am forever thankful to my parents and sisters for always pushing me to reach for the stars.